When Someone you love has passed away,
It's OK to miss them or be sad they aren't here.
When you share stories of their life with others,
Their memory lives on, keeping them close and
near.

In Loving Memory
of Brady Meier
Forever in our
Hearts

This is Brady.

He had orange hair and a big smile.

*He loved to freestyle walk...*
*mile*
*after mile.*

He loved his Tucker.

He loved to sing.

He loved to build things.

WOOOOO HOOOOO!

He loved to ski.

He loved to try new things.

He loved
to dance
without care.

He loved to say–

He loved his Cadillac.

He loved his friends and family...

...and we all loved him back!

Archway Publishing books may be ordered through booksellers or by contacting:

Archway Publishing
1663 Liberty Drive
Bloomington, IN 47403
www.archwaypublishing.com
1 (888) 242-5904

ISBN: 978-1-4808-8272-0 (sc)
ISBN: 978-1-4808-8271-3 (e)

Print information available on the last page.

Archway Publishing rev. date: 09/18/2019

Printed in the United States
By Bookmasters